SAMPLE COLORING PAGES

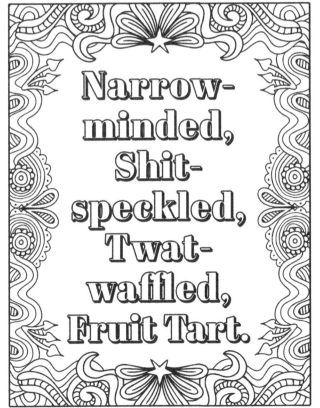

Shove it Up Your Fucking Ass!

EXTRA Stress-relieving designs!

Do you need to take the edge off? This coloring book is jam-packed with EXTRA stress-relieving designs to help you relax and unwind! Perfect gift too!

AVAILABLE ON AMAZON.COM!

SEARCH FOR: Shove it up your fucking ass + John T

Sign Up Now!

Go to **SwearWordColoringBook.com** and sign up to my mailing list for news, updates, and FREE coloring pages!

This SPECIAL EDITION Adult Coloring Book is divided
into THREE sections:

～1～

20 of my BEST adult coloring pages
from the following titles:

Make Life Your Bitch
Fucksicles
Greetings...Asshole!
Can't Fix Stupid!
Eat, Shit, & Die
Just Calm the Fuck Down
Strange Paradise
Bah Fucking Humbug
Sweary Xmas & a Nasty New Year!

Look at the back of the coloring page for the title of the book.
Search (Title + John T) on Amazon.com

～2～

20 BRAND NEW adult coloring pages

A variety of adult coloring pages with swear words and phrases.

～3～

10 QUARANTINE EDITION adult coloring pages

A variety of adult coloring pages to help you color away pandemic chaos!

Happy Fucking Coloring.

Make Life Your Bitch

Make Life Your Bitch

Make Life Your Bitch

Make Life Your Bitch

Fucksicles

Fucksicles

Sweary and tasty.

Fucksicles

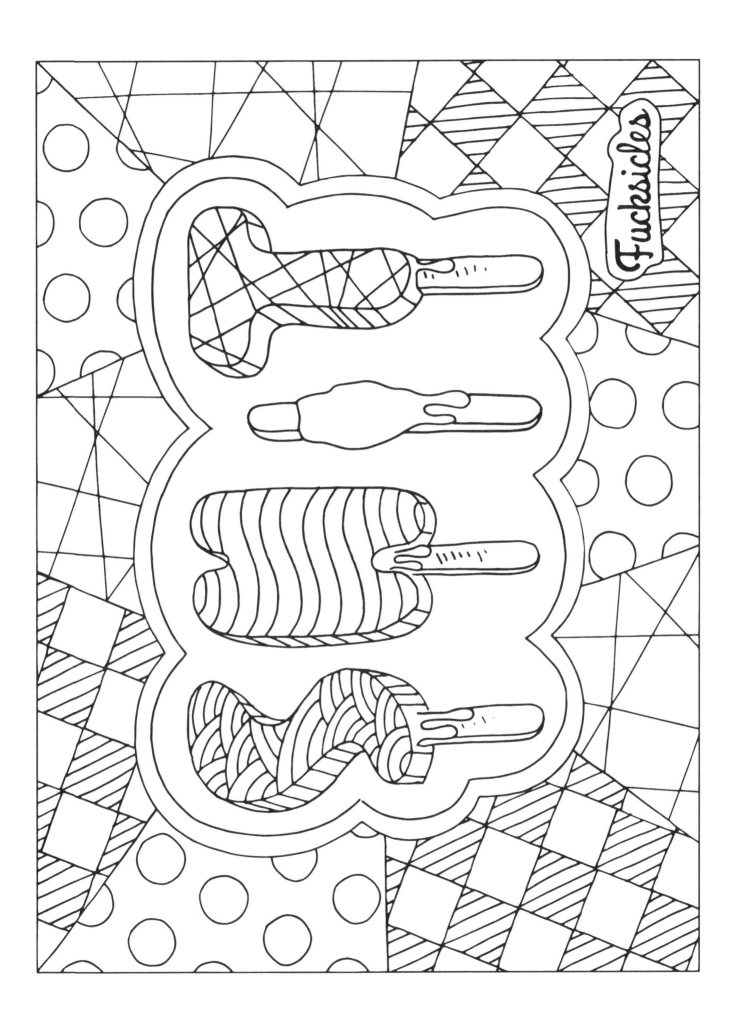

Fucksicles

Greetings...Asshole!

Greetings...Asshole!

Greetings...Asshole!

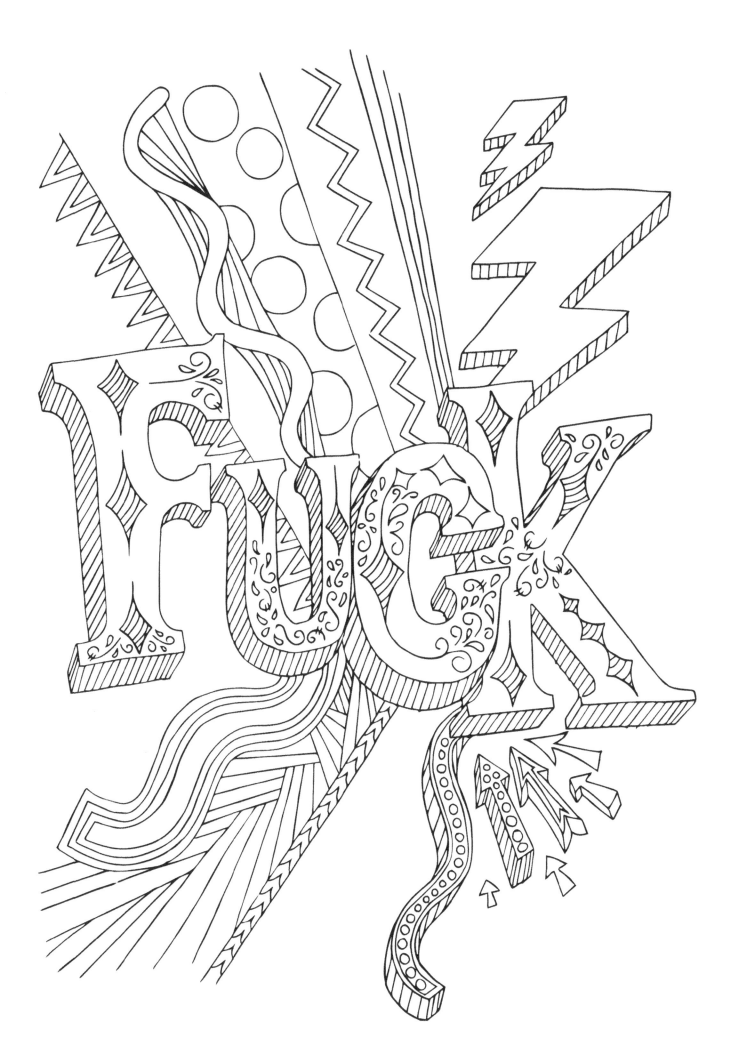

Can't Fix Stupid!

Can't Fix Stupid!

Eat Shit & Die

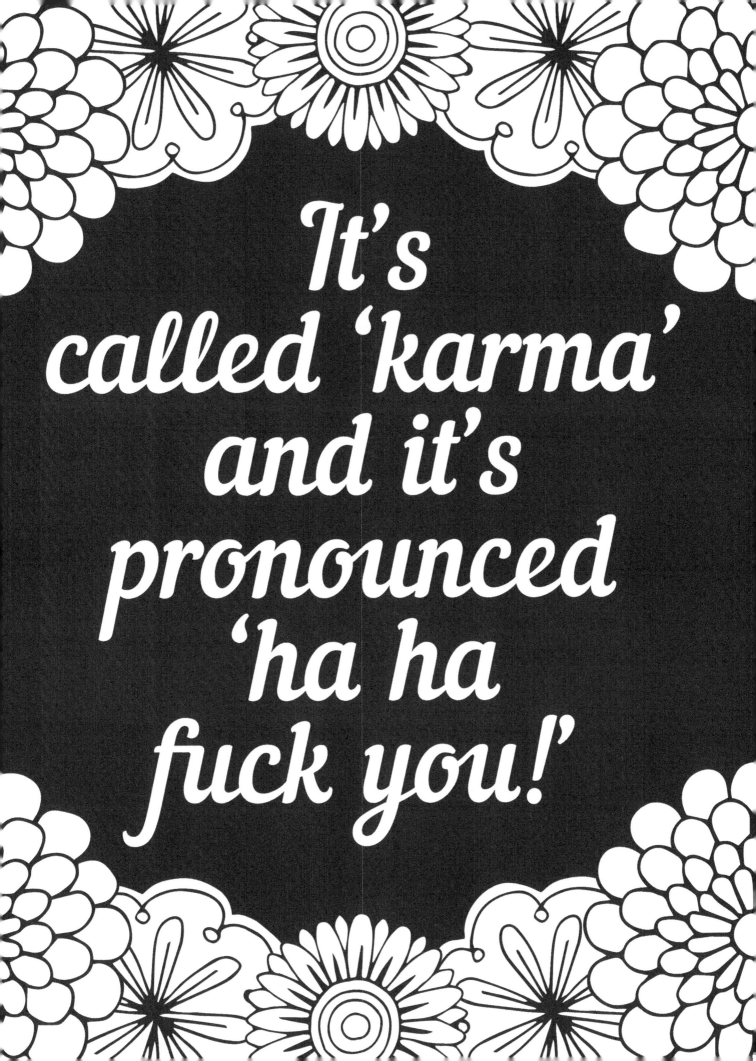

Just Calm the F*ck Down

Just Calm the F*ck Down

Strange Paradise

(for a shittier result, don't use scissors, just tear!)

COLOR YOUR OWN FUCKING CARD.

Shitty Xmas card

Color, cutout, fold, & give!

FUCK you.

Bah Fucking Humbug!

Bah Fucking Humbug!

Sweary Xmas & a Nasty New Year

Sweary Xmas & a Nasty New Year

New Coloring Pages.

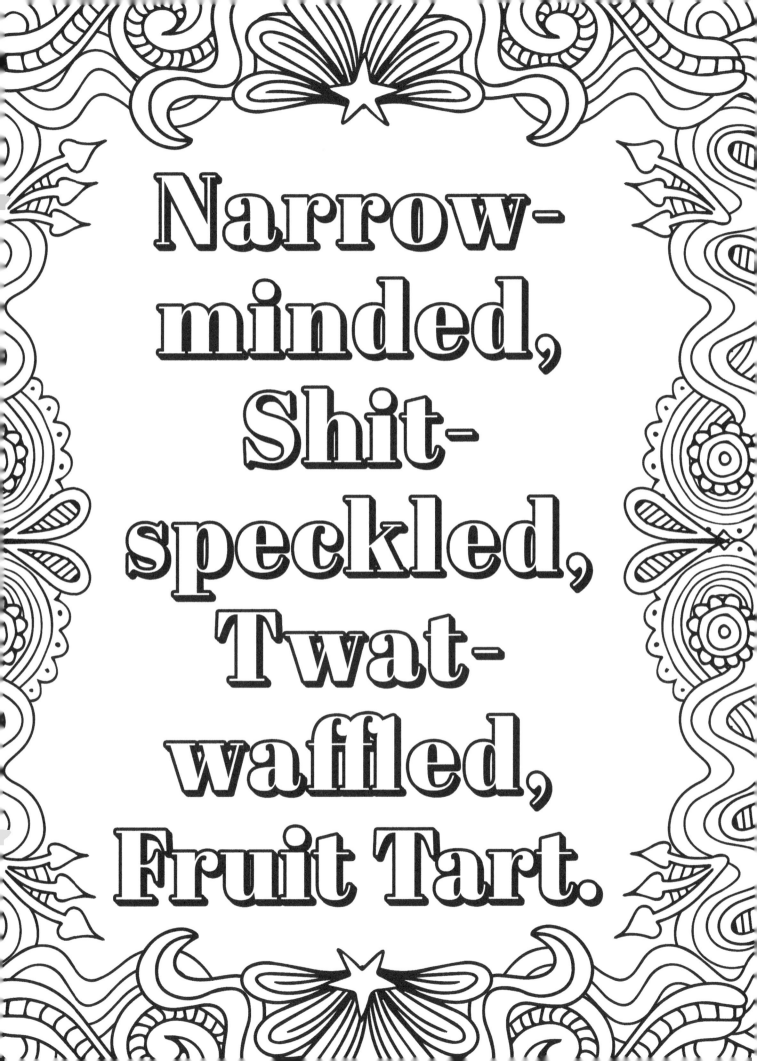

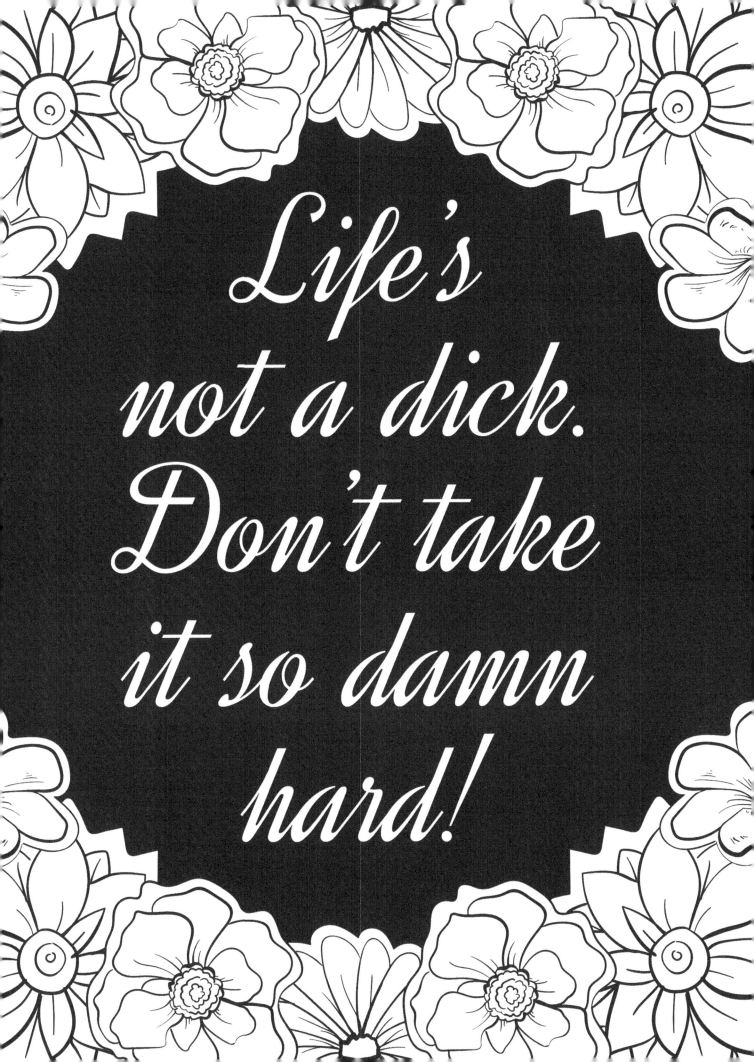

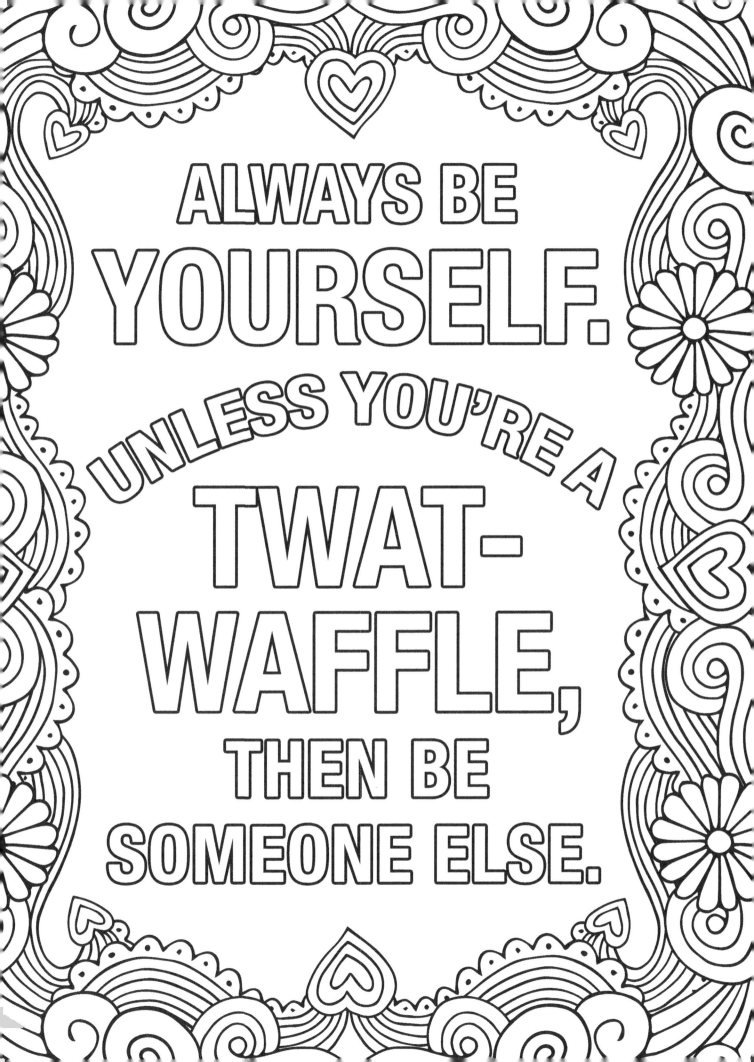

Stop
hoarding
everything,
asshole!

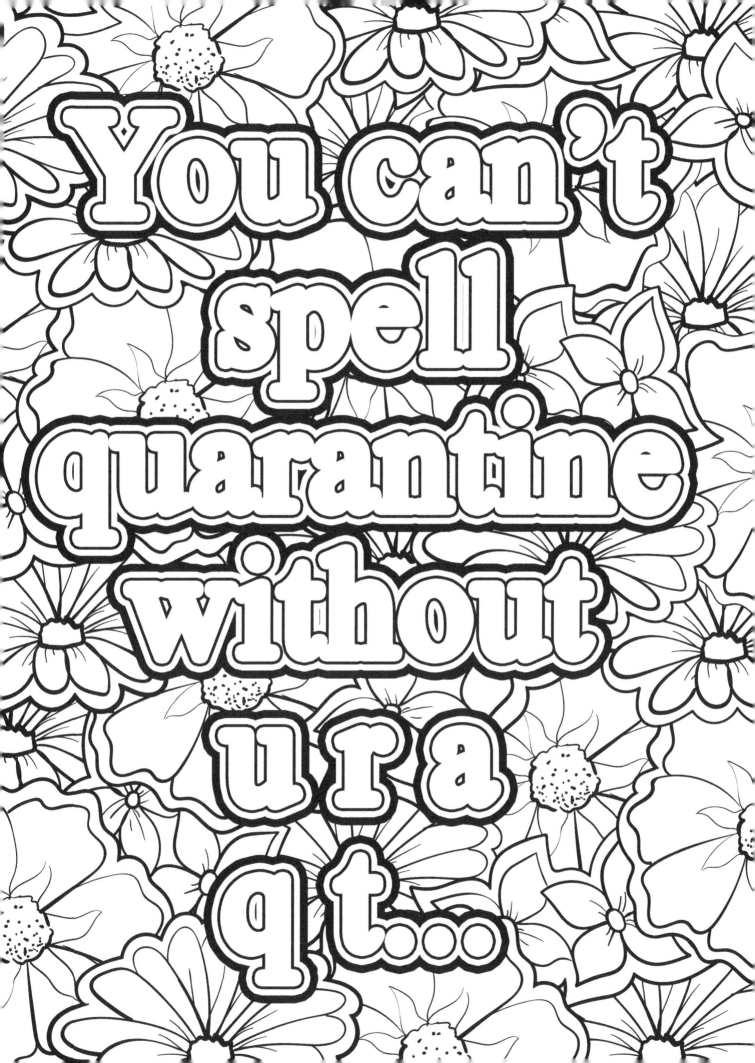

Made in the USA
Monee, IL
31 March 2022